THE TALE
OF
MR. JEREMY FISHER

THE TALE OF

MR. JEREMY FISHER

BY

BEATRIX POTTER

Author of
" The Tale of Peter Rabbit," &c.

FREDERICK WARNE

*The reproductions in this book have been made using
the most modern electronic scanning methods from entirely
new transparencies of Beatrix Potter's original watercolours.
They enable Beatrix Potter's skill as an artist to be appreciated
as never before, not even during her own lifetime.*

FREDERICK WARNE

Published by the Penguin Group
27 Wrights Lane, London w8 5tz, England
Viking Penguin Inc., 40 West 23rd Street, New York, New York 10010, USA
Penguin Books Australia Ltd, Ringwood, Victoria, Australia
Penguin Books Canada Ltd, 2801 John Street, Markham, Ontario, Canada l3r 1b4
Penguin Books (NZ) Ltd, 182–190 Wairau Road, Auckland 10, New Zealand

Penguin Books Ltd, Registered Offices: Harmondsworth, Middlesex, England

First published 1906
This edition with new reproductions first published 1987
This impression 1989

Colour reproduction by
East Anglian Engraving Company Ltd, Norwich
Printed and bound in Great Britain by
William Clowes Limited, Beccles and London

FOR
STEPHANIE
FROM
COUSIN B.

ONCE upon a time there was a frog called Mr. Jeremy Fisher ; he lived in a little damp house amongst the buttercups at the edge of a pond.

THE water was all slippy-sloppy in the larder and in the back passage.

But Mr. Jeremy liked getting his feet wet; nobody ever scolded him, and he never caught a cold!

HE was quite pleased when he looked out and saw large drops of rain, splashing in the pond—

"I WILL get some worms and go fishing and catch a dish of minnows for my dinner," said Mr. Jeremy Fisher. "If I catch more than five fish, I will invite my friends Mr. Alderman Ptolemy Tortoise and Sir Isaac Newton. The Alderman, however, eats salad."

M R. JEREMY put on a
macintosh, and a pair
of shiny goloshes ; he took his
rod and basket, and set off
with enormous hops to the
place where he kept his boat.

THE boat was round and green, and very like the other lily-leaves. It was tied to a water-plant in the middle of the pond.

MR. JEREMY took a reed pole, and pushed the boat out into open water. "I know a good place for minnows," said Mr. Jeremy Fisher.

MR. JEREMY stuck his pole into the mud and fastened his boat to it.

Then he settled himself cross-legged and arranged his fishing tackle. He had the dearest little red float. His rod was a tough stalk of grass, his line was a fine long white horse-hair, and he tied a little wriggling worm at the end.

THE rain trickled down his back, and for nearly an hour he stared at the float.

"This is getting tiresome, I think I should like some lunch," said Mr. Jeremy Fisher.

HE punted back again amongst the water-plants, and took some lunch out of his basket.

"I will eat a butterfly sandwich, and wait till the shower is over," said Mr. Jeremy Fisher.

A GREAT big water-beetle came up underneath the lily leaf and tweaked the toe of one of his goloshes.

Mr. Jeremy crossed his legs up shorter, out of reach, and went on eating his sandwich.

ONCE or twice something moved about with a rustle and a splash amongst the rushes at the side of the pond.

"I trust that is not a rat," said Mr. Jeremy Fisher; " I think I had better get away from here."

MR. JEREMY shoved the boat out again a little way, and dropped in the bait. There was a bite almost directly; the float gave a tremendous bobbit!

"A minnow! a minnow! I have him by the nose!" cried Mr. Jeremy Fisher, jerking up his rod.

BUT what a horrible sur-
prise! Instead of a
smooth fat minnow, Mr.
Jeremy landed little Jack
Sharp the stickleback, covered
with spines!

THE stickleback floundered
about the boat, pricking
and snapping until he was
quite out of breath. Then he
jumped back into the water.

AND a shoal of other little fishes put their heads out, and laughed at Mr. Jeremy Fisher.

AND while Mr. Jeremy sat disconsolately on the edge of his boat—sucking his sore fingers and peering down into the water—a *much* worse thing happened; a really *frightful* thing it would have been, if Mr. Jeremy had not been wearing a macintosh!

A GREAT big enormous trout came up—ker-pflop-p-p-p! with a splash—and it seized Mr. Jeremy with a snap, "Ow! Ow! Ow!"—and then it turned and dived down to the bottom of the pond!

BUT the trout was so displeased with the taste of the macintosh, that in less than half a minute it spat him out again; and the only thing it swallowed was Mr. Jeremy's goloshes.

MR. JEREMY bounced up
to the surface of the
water, like a cork and the
bubbles out of a soda water
bottle; and he swam with
all his might to the edge of
the pond.

HE scrambled out on the first bank he came to, and he hopped home across the meadow with his macintosh all in tatters.

"WHAT a mercy that was not a pike!" said Mr. Jeremy Fisher. "I have lost my rod and basket; but it does not much matter, for I am sure I should never have dared to go fishing again!"

HE put some sticking
plaster on his fingers,
and his friends both came to
dinner. He could not offer
them fish, but he had something else in his larder.

SIR ISAAC NEWTON
wore his black and gold
waistcoat,

AND Mr. Alderman Ptolemy Tortoise brought a salad with him in a string bag.

AND instead of a nice dish of minnows—they had a roasted grasshopper with lady-bird sauce; which frogs consider a beautiful treat; but *I* think it must have been nasty!

THE END